W9-AEG-062

To Angel and the Crampo Kid

and with special thanks to Barbara Lalicki

Printed in the United States of America.   First Edition   3   4   5   6   7   8   9   10

Library of Congress Cataloging in Publication Data
Cummings, Pat. Jimmy Lee did it. Summary: Artie keeps telling his sister that the messes all over their house
are the work of the elusive Jimmy Lee.
1. Children's stories, American.   [1. Brothers—Fiction.   2. Afro-Americans—Fiction.   3. Stories in rhyme]
I. Title.   PZ8.3.C898Ji   1985   [E]   84-21322   ISBN 0-688-04632-0   ISBN 0-688-04633-9 (lib. bdg.)

JIMMY LEE DID IT

BY PAT CUMMINGS

LOTHROP, LEE & SHEPARD BOOKS
New York

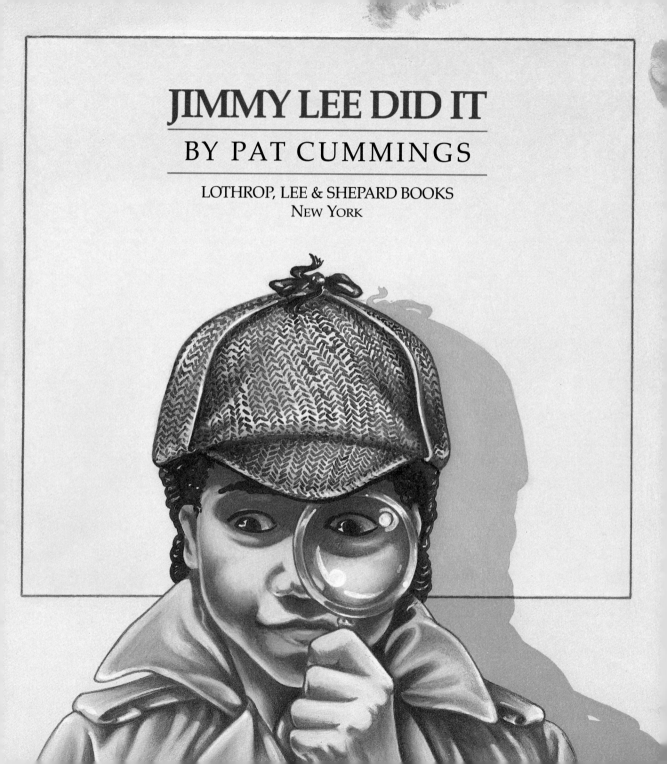

Jimmy Lee is back again
And nothing is the same.

He's causing lots of trouble,
While my brother takes the blame.

Artie made his bed, he said.
But Jimmy thinks he's smart.

While Artie read his comics,
Jimmy pulled the sheets apart.

Dad fixed us pancakes
And Artie said his tasted fine,

But Jimmy Lee had just been there
And eaten most of mine.

I heard the crash of breaking glass,
But turned too late, I guess.

"Jimmy Lee did it," Artie said,
As we cleaned up the mess.

When Artie's room got painted,
Jimmy Lee was in the hall.

He used up Artie's crayons
Drawing pictures on the wall.

And when I finally found my bear,
I asked Artie, "Who hid it?"

He told me frankly, "Angel,
It was Jimmy Lee who did it."

He caused so much trouble
That I began to see—

The only way to stop it
Was to capture Jimmy Lee.

I knew about his sweet tooth,
So I set a tasty trap,

But Jimmy Lee just waited
Till I had to take my nap.

I spread out all my marbles
To trip up Jimmy Lee.

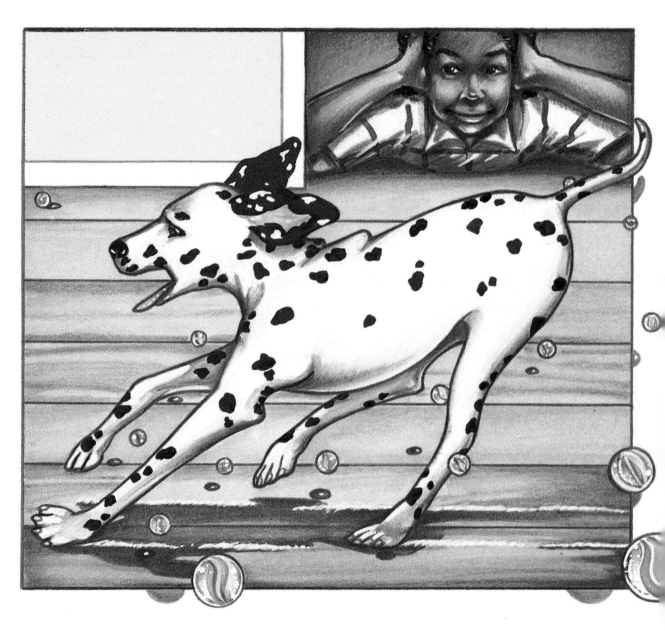

The dog slid by and scratched the floor
And Mom got mad at me.

I hid in the hall closet
And I never made a sound,

But Jimmy Lee will only come
When Artie is around.

I don't know what he looks like,
He never leaves a trace—

Except for spills and tears
And Artie's things about the place.

Since Artie won't describe him,
He remains a mystery.

But if you're smart, you'll listen
And watch out for Jimmy Lee.